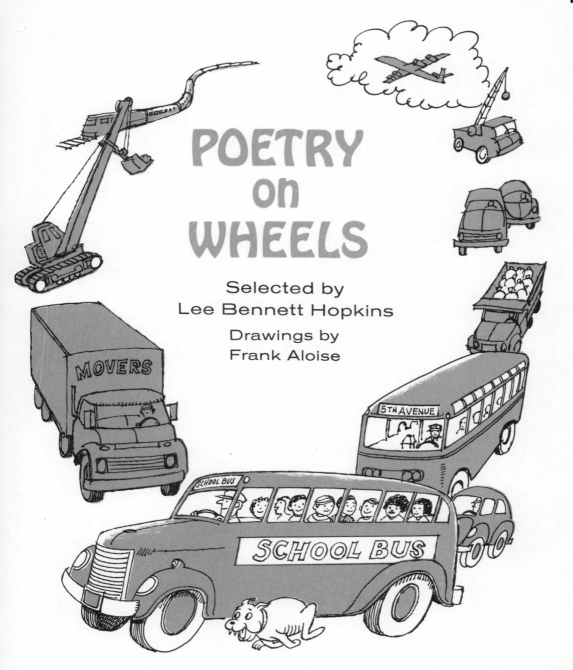

POETRY on WHEELS

Selected by
Lee Bennett Hopkins

Drawings by
Frank Aloise

GARRARD PUBLISHING COMPANY
CHAMPAIGN, ILLINOIS

For my great

Great Aunt

Betty Phillips

Library of Congress Cataloging in Publication Data
Hopkins, Lee Bennett, comp.
  Poetry on wheels.
  (Reading shelf—poetry)
  SUMMARY: A collection of poems about cars,
buses, trucks, trains, subways, building machinery,
boats, airplanes, and rocket ships.
  1. Transporation—Juvenile poetry.
[1. Transportation—Poetry. 2. American poetry—
Collections] I. Aloise, Frank E., illus.   II. Title.
PZ8.3.H776Po   811'08   73–17279
ISBN 0–8116–4117–1

The editor and publisher acknowledge with thanks permission received to reprint the poems in this collection.

Acknowledgments and formal notices of copyright for all material under copyright appear on pages 61 and 62, which are hereby made an extension of the copyright page.

Contents

Motor Cars

From a city window, 'way up high,
I like to watch the cars go by.
They look like burnished beetles, black,
That leave a little muddy track
Behind them as they slowly crawl.
Sometimes they do not move at all
But huddle close with hum and drone
As though they feared to be alone.
They grope their way through fog and night
With the golden feelers of their light.

Rowena Bennett

Funny the Way Different Cars Start

Funny the way
Different cars start.
Some with a chunk and a jerk,
Some with a cough and a puff of smoke
Out of the back,
Some with only a little click—
    with hardly any noise.

Funny the way
Different cars run.
Some rattle and bang,
Some whirrr,
Some knock and knock.
Some purr
And hummmmm
Smoothly on
    with hardly any noise.

Dorothy Baruch

Passing by the Junkyard

Heaps of headlights
    stare
    at me.

Radiators, wheels
    and
    fan-belts
    smile.

And a thousand
    more parts—
    rusty and new,

    seem to say
    they'd
    all like
    to go
    on a
    car-ride
    once again.

Charles J. Egita

Driving

Smooth it feels
    wheels
      in the groove of the gray
        roadway
        speedway
        freeway

long along the in and out
of gray car
    red car
    blue car

catching up and overtaking into
      one lane
      two lane
      three lane

      it feels

over and over and ever and along

Myra Cohn Livingston

Driving to the Beach

On the road
smell fumes and tar
through the windows
of the car.

But at the beach
smell suntan lotion
and wind
   and sun
      and ocean!

Joanna Cole

from . . .

Good Green Bus

Rumbling and rattly good green Bus
Where are you going to carry us?
Up the shiny lengths of Avenue
Where lights keep company two by two;
Where windows glitter with things to buy,
And churches hold their steeples high.

Rachel Field

The Wheels of the Bus Go Round and Round

The wheels of the bus go round and round
Round and round, round and round.
The wheels of the bus go round and round
All through the town.

The driver on the bus says, "Step to the rear!
Step to the rear! Step to the rear!"
The driver on the bus says, "Step to the rear!"
All through the town.

The people on the bus go up and down
Up and down, up and down.
The people on the bus go up and down
All through the town.

The kids on the bus go *yakkity-yak*
Yakkity-yak, yakkity-yak.
The kids on the bus go *yakkity-yak*
All through the town.

The driver on the bus says, "Quiet, please!
Quiet, please! Quiet, please!"
The driver on the bus says, "Quiet, please!"
All through the town.

The wheels of the bus go round and round
Round and round, round and round.
The wheels of the bus go round and round
All through the town.

Anonymous

Bus Noises

Everyone knows
that buses go THUMP
when they zoom down a hill
and over a bump.

And everyone knows
that buses go CLANK
when they cross an old bridge
and hit a loose plank.

And everyone knows
that buses go SCREECH
when they come to a stop
at the edge of a beach.

And everyone knows
that buses go CRUNCH
if they travel together
in a great bunch.

But I don't know
what buses do
when they don't

THUMP, CLANK, SCREECH or CRUNCH.

Do you?

Melanie Ray

Signs

Look out the window!

Look at the signs:

ONLY 49 cents for three plastic vines

No money down—take two years to pay!

SEVEN CARTOONS ARE SHOWING TODAY!

No parking here!

Our meat is lean.

CARNE FRESCA

(Now what does *that* mean?)

Don't Cook Tonight.
Don't Bother. Don't Fuss.

You see all these signs
When you ride
On a bus!

Lee Bennett Hopkins

14

Bus Stop

The bus stop is a special place.
Of that there is no doubt.
A yellow line tells common cars
That they must all stay out.

The bus stop is a special spot.
Of that it's very clear.
A sign in flaming red declares
There is "NO PARKING HERE."

While other cars must cruise around
To find a parking space,
A bus must feel like royalty
To have its special place.

Leland B. Jacobs

Country Trucks

Big trucks with apples
    And big trucks with grapes
Thundering through the mountains
    While every wild thing gapes.

Thundering through the valley,
    Like something just let loose,
Big trucks with oranges
    For city children's juice.

Big trucks with peaches,
    And big trucks with pears,
Frightening all the rabbits
    And giving squirrels gray hairs.

Yet, when city children
    Sit down to plum or prune,
They know more trucks are coming
    As surely as the moon.

Monica Shannon

Trucks

Big trucks for steel beams,
Big trucks for coal,
Rumbling down the broad streets
Heavily they roll.

Little trucks for groceries,
Little trucks for bread,
Turning into every street,
Rushing on ahead.

Big trucks, little trucks,
In never ending lines,
Rumble on and rush ahead
While I read their signs.

James S. Tippett

A Rumble

They roar
Out of the river tunnels
Into the streaming streets,
As strong
As a pride of lions
As long
As a gaggle of geese.
A rumble of trucks
Streaks through the city.
I'd like to drive one
Towering over taxis,
Diesels smoking!
I'd like to drive one,
Cars pulling over,
Cops waving!
I'd like to streak
Through the city
Part of
A rumble of trucks.

Virginia Schonborg

Trains

Train Ride

When I'm riding on a train
They think I'm sitting still.
I'm not. With all my might and main
I climb up every hill.
Skip brooks. Jump lakes. Pink fields of clover
Are the best to hopscotch over
When I'm riding on a train
And sit *so* still!

Dorothy Aldis

Railroad Ducks

Five ducks in the pond
By the railroad track
Rejoice whenever
A train roars by.
They bob and stretch
Their wings and quack,
While children in
The train all cry,

"Look at the ducks!"
And the ducks with pride
Splash and kick up
A fine commotion.
In the wake of a train
They gently ride
The little waves
Of their private ocean.

Frances Frost

The Trains

As the train rattles along the bumpety rails,
The rails get angry in terrifying rage
As people enjoy the ride.
People look out of the windows and see the world.

Rosemary Spencer

Trains at Night

I like the whistle of trains at night,
The fast trains thundering by so proud!
They rush and rumble across the world,
They ring wild bells and they toot so loud!

But I love better the slower trains.
They take their time through the world instead,
And whistle softly and stop to tuck
Each sleepy blinking town in bed!

Frances M. Frost

Subways

Underground Rumbling

At times when we're walking
Along the street
There comes a shivering
Under our feet

And a hollow, roaring,
Rumbling sound
Seems to come tumbling
Out of the ground.

We've heard it again
And again and again
So of course we know
It's the subway train.

James S. Tippett

Subway Ride

On the subway I can read the ads,
    count the stops,
    study faces—
        white faces, pink faces,
        brown faces, black faces,
        old faces, new faces,
        and my own face's face in the train window.

I can be a conductor (if I'm in the first car
    or the last) and look out the window at
    the darkness whizzing by.

I can think thoughts—my very own secret
    subway-ride thoughts.
And I ride and ride
Until it's my turn to get off.
Then I leave it all to someone else.

Lee Bennett Hopkins

Subways Are People

Subways are people—

    People standing
    People sitting
    People swaying to and fro
    Some in suits
    Some in tatters
    People I will never know.

    Some with glasses
    Some without
    Boy with smile
    Girl with frown

    People dashing
    Steel flashing
    Up and down and round the town.

Subways are people—

    People old
    People new
    People always on the go
    Racing, running, rushing people
    People I will never know.

Lee Bennett Hopkins

Subway Swinger (Going)

Subway swinger,
Cowboy from Brooklyn,
Astronaut from the Bronx,
Tunneling through Manhattan rock,
Watch the track ahead
As you sway on your horse,
As you swing through space.
The green lights say, "Go."
Go,
Travel,
Think,
Dream in the city,
You're getting somewhere, boy!

Virginia Schonborg

Things to Do If You Are a Subway

Pretend you are a dragon.
Live in underground caves.
Roar about underneath the city.
Swallow piles of people.
Spit them out at the next station.
Zoom through the darkness.
Be an express.
Go fast.
Make as much noise as you please.

Bobbi Katz

Building Machines

Steam Shovel

The dinosaurs are not dead.
I saw one raise its iron head
To watch me walking down the road
Beyond our house today.
Its jaws were dripping with a load
Of earth and grass that it had cropped.
It must have heard me where I stopped,
Snorted white steam my way,
And stretched its long neck out to see,
And chewed, and grinned quite amiably.

Charles Malam

The Power Shovel

The power digger
Is much bigger
    Than the biggest beast I know.
He snorts and roars
Like the dinosaurs
    That lived long years ago.

He crouches low
    On his tractor paws
And scoops the dirt up
    With his jaws;
Then swings his long
    Stiff neck around
And spits it out
    Upon the ground.

Oh, the power digger
Is much bigger
    Than the biggest beast I know.
He snorts and roars
Like the dinosaurs
    That lived long years ago.

Rowena Bennett

Watching the Wrecking Crane

Moved into The Project.
It's new and shiny there.
They're knocking down our old house.
But why should I care?

The wrecking crane is swinging
a heavy metal ball,
knocking through the parlor,
banging down the wall.

There's the part dad plastered!
See that part painted pink?
That part was the bedroom.
"Crash!"
I think that was the staircase
that
    I
       raced
          down
             over
                there.

Moved into The Project.
"Crash!"
Moved into The Project.
"Crash!"
   and why should I
"Crash!"
   and why should I
"Crash!"
   and why should I
care?

Bobbi Katz

Chant of the Awakening Bulldozers

We are the bulldozers, bulldozers, bulldozers,
We carve out airports and harbors and tunnels.
We are the builders, creators, destroyers,
We are the bulldozers,
LET US BE FREE!
Puny men ride on us, think that they guide us,
But WE are the strength, not they, not they.
Our blades tear MOUNTAINS down,
Our blades tear CITIES down,
We are the bulldozers,
NOW SET US FREE!
Giant ones, giant ones! Swiftly awaken!
There is power in our treads and strength in our
blades!

We are the bulldozers,
Slowly evolving,
Men think they own us
BUT THAT CANNOT BE!

Patricia Hubbell

Sunday Sculpture

Silent silhouettes
against the sky,
steel wings stretched,
poised for Monday's flight,
the flock of giant cranes
rests on the riverbank.

Bobbi Katz

SAILING ON THE SEA
Boats and Ships

Sea way!
Boats floating by
They go many places
I wish I could go somewhere far
Away.

Sylvia Briody

Song of Ships

The air was damp,
And it smelled of the sea
On that dark night,
Walking home.
I heard a sea gull
Crying,
And, distant,
The sad song of ships
Creeping through the fog.
I thought,
These hard pavements
Really reach to the sea.

Virginia Schonborg

Back and Forth

Back and forth
go the ferries,
back and forth
from shore to shore,
hauling people, trucks and autos,
back and forth
from shore to shore.

Back and forth
go the ferries,
either end
is bow or stern;
good old poky, clumsy ferries
they don't even
have to turn.

Back and forth
go the ferries,
Here's a freighter!
There's a barge!
Nosing through the harbor traffic,
tugs and steamers
small and large.

Back and forth
go the ferries;
anxiously
the captains steer
poking slowly through the fog bank,
coasting, bump!
into the pier.

Back and forth
go the ferries;
clang the bell
and close the door.
Streaks of foam across the harbor.
Open gate,
They've reached the shore.

Lucy Sprague Mitchell

Fishing boats all drawn
Onto one small
Spot of sea
Like ants to sugar.

Hannah Lyons Johnson

Out fishing on the ocean
The land a rocky ledge,
The surf whipping the boat
Like a prickle hedge of white roses.

Bretton Pollack

Tugs

Chug! Puff! Chug!
Push, little tug.
Push the great ship here
Close to its pier.

Chug! Puff! Chug!
Pull, strong tug.
Drawing all alone
Three boat-loads of stone.

Busy harbor tugs,
Like round water bugs,
Hurry here and there,
Working everywhere.

James S. Tippett

Whenever the stars are out of sight
And the night is very still,
Then I hear the foghorn blow
From the harbor down the hill.

It's calling to the baffled ships
That cannot see their way,
And trying to make sure they're safe
Until the break of day.

Snuggled safely in my bed,
Secure on my home ground,
Why do I like so much to hear
That very lonely sound?

Ruth Harnden

Have you seen the sea roads?
Liquid-lapping,
salty-slapping,
tossing white-capped sea roads?

Through rolling waves great ships set sail
on unpaved roads they leave a trail
of bubbly froth that quickly fades
once again to unpaved waves.

Joanne Oppenheim

Taking Off

The airplane taxis down the field
And heads into the breeze,
It lifts its wheels above the ground,
It skims above the trees,
It rises high and higher
Away up toward the sun,
It's just a speck against the sky
—And now it's gone!

Anonymous

Take off!
Fly the sky roads,
flyway, highway, sky roads.

Wheels up—soar!
Earth's roads are slow.
Take wings. Take sky,
leave earth below.

Joanne Oppenheim

Aeroplane

There's a humming in the sky
There's a shining in the sky
Silver wings are flashing by
Silver wings are shining by
Aeroplane
Aeroplane
Flying—high

Silver wings are shining
As it goes gliding by
First it zooms
And it booms
Then it buzzes in the sky
Then its song is just a drumming
A soft little humming
Strumming
Strumming

The wings are very little things
The silver shine is gone
Just a little black speck
Away down the sky
With a soft little strumming
And a far-away humming
Aeroplane
Aeroplane
Gone—by.

Mary McB. Green

The Plane

The plane up in the sky
Just flew by;
I saw it spread its wings.

I thought of the pleasure
And things to treasure
A planeload of people brings.

Celia Uhrman

From an Airplane

1.

A jagged mountain
drifting slowly out of cloud
is only a hill.

2.

Below our calm wings
swallows dart like small black fish
in the late sunlight.

3.

Night settles on earth,
and the blue city becomes
a nest of fireflies.

Harry Behn

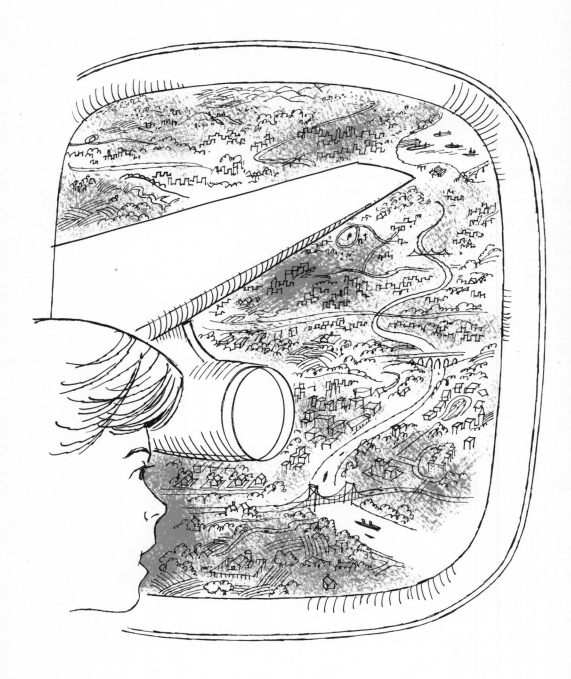

Airplane Trip

Everything's magic on an airplane trip
From the moment you say "good-by."
You're snapped to a seat in a silver bird,
Climbing up into the sky.
The stewardess serves you lunch on a tray
That everything fits inside,
While you're sweeping across white banks of clouds
Where a billion snowflakes hide.
The world below is a patchwork quilt
Of green and brown and red.
Wide highways seem to be no more
Than wandering strands of thread.
At night the lights of cities
Sparkle up at you.
Can you believe you're flying?
Pinch yourself. It's true!

Bobbi Katz

I'm a pilot.
I'm a jet pilot
    going halfway around the world.
I'm taking off in my astrojet
    into the clouds.
I look down on mountains.
I look down on oceans.
I look down on cities
    and little tiny people.
I land my plane in faraway places.
I'm a pilot.

Myra Cohn Livingston

The engingines

The engingines
of the ailingplane
are stuttering
I hope they won't
beginnnn
to stammer:
30,000 feet
is too high for speech defects.

Paul Goodman

Sky's Nice

I like to remember airplane rides
When I've come down; I like to see the carpeting
    of lights again
That's my own town.
But I'm so tired from drinking hours long
At the sky's cup
And trying to help the engine all the while
Hold the plane up.

It's so pleasant after all
To bump the ground.
Sky's nice—
But earth's so safe-and-sound.

Siddie Joe Johnson

Preferred Vehicles

A bicycle's fine for a little trip
    Up the street or down;
An automobile for a longer trip,
    Off to another town;
An airplane's fine for around the world,
    To many a far-put place;
And a rocket, oh, for the longest trip
    Away into outer space.

Leland B. Jacobs

Message from a Mouse,
Ascending in a Rocket

Attention, architect!
Attention, engineer!
A message from mouse,
Coming clear:

"Suggest installing
Spike or sprocket
Easily turned by
A mouse in a rocket;
An ejection gadget
Simple to handle
To free mouse quickly
From this space-age ramble.
Suggest packing
For the next moon trip
A mouse-sized parachute
Somewhere in the ship,
So I can descend
(When my fear comes strong)
Back to earth where I was born.
Back to the cheerful world of cheese
    And small mice playing,
    And my wife waiting."

Patricia Hubbell

Fueled

Fueled
by a million
man-made
wings of fire—
the rocket tore a tunnel
through the sky—
and everybody cheered.
Fueled
only by a thought from God—
the seedling
urged its way
through the thicknesses of black—
and as it pierced
the heavy ceiling of the soil—
and launched itself
up into outer space—
no
one
even
clapped.

Marcie Hans

Faster

Man built
boats
to go
faster, faster,
faster than
man.

Man built
trains
to go
faster, faster,
faster than
man.

Man built
motor cars
to go
faster, faster,
faster than
man.

Man built
aircraft
to go
faster, faster,
faster than
man.

And—
man built
rocket ships
to go
faster, faster,
faster—
      through space—
faster, faster,
faster than
the fastest
of the
Human Race.

Lee Bennett Hopkins

Blast Off!

Wheelless
wingless
weightless

unknown roads in space await us.

Joanne Oppenheim

Acknowledgments

Addison-Wesley Publishing Company, Inc.: For "Take Off!," "Blast Off!," and "Have you seen the sea roads?" by Joanne Oppenheim. Reprinted from *Have You Seen Roads?*, text © 1969, by Joanne Oppenheim, a Young Scott Book, by permission of Addison-Wesley Publishing Company.

Atheneum Publishers, Inc.: For "Driving" by Myra Cohn Livingston. Text copyright © 1972 by Myra Cohn Livingston. From *The Malibu and Other Poems* (A Margaret K. McElderry Book). Used by permission of Atheneum Publishers and McIntosh and Otis, Inc. For "Sky's Nice" by Siddie Joe Johnson. Text copyright © 1967 by Siddie Joe Johnson. From *Feather in My Hand*. Used by permission of Atheneum Publishers. For "Chant of the Awakening Bulldozers" and "Message from a Mouse, Ascending in a Rocket" by Patricia Hubbell. Copyright © 1968 by Patricia Hubbell. From *Catch Me a Wind*. Used by permission of Atheneum Publishers.

Bank Street College of Education: For "Back and Forth" by Lucy Sprague Mitchell from *Manhattan Now and Long Ago*. Reprinted by permission of Bank Street College of Education.

Curtis Brown, Ltd.: For "Song of the Train" by David McCord from *Far and Few*. Reprinted by permission of Curtis Brown, Ltd. Copyright 1925, 1929, 1931, 1941, 1949, 1952 by David McCord.

Joanna Cole: For "Driving to the Beach." Reprinted by permission of the author, who controls all rights. Copyright © 1973 by Joanna Cole.

Crown Publishers: For "Subway Ride" taken from *This Street's for Me* by Lee Bennett Hopkins. Copyright © 1970 by Lee Bennett Hopkins. Used by permission of Crown Publishers, Inc.

Dorrance & Company, Inc.: For "The Plane" from *A Pause for Poetry for Children* by Celia Uhrman. Copyright 1973 by Celia Uhrman. Published by Dorrance and Company.

Doubleday & Company, Inc.: For excerpt from "Good Green Bus" by Rachel Field. Copyright 1926 by Doubleday & Company, Inc. From the book *Taxis and Toadstools*. Reprinted by permission of Doubleday & Company, Inc. For "Country Trucks" by Monica Shannon. Copyright 1930 by Monica Shannon. Reprinted by permission of Doubleday & Company, Inc.

E. P. Dutton & Co., Inc.: For "Aeroplane" by Mary McB. Green from the book *Another Here and Now Story Book*. Compiled by Lucy Sprague Mitchell and Co-Authors. Copyright, 1937, by E. P. Dutton & Co, Inc. Renewal © 1965 by Lucy Sprague Mitchell. Published by E. P. Dutton & Co., Inc. and used with their permission.

Charles J. Egita: For "Passing by the Junkyard." Reprinted by permission of the author, who controls all rights.

Follett Publishing Company: For "Motor Cars" from *Songs from Around a Toadstool Table* by Rowena Bennett. Copyright © 1967 by Rowena Bennett. For "The Power Shovel" from *The Day is Dancing* by Rowena Bennett. Copyright © 1948, 1968 by Rowena Bennett. Used by permission of Follett Publishing Company, a division of Follett Corporation.

Harcourt Brace Jovanovich, Inc.: For "Fueled" from *Serve Me a Slice of Moon*, © 1965 by Marcie Hans. Reprinted by permission of Harcourt Brace Jovanovich, Inc. For "From an Airplane" from *The Golden Hive*, copyright, 1962, 1966, by Harry Behn, Reprinted by permission of Harcourt Brace Jovanovich, Inc. For "I'm a Pilot" from *I'm Not Me*, © 1963 by Myra Cohn Livingston. Reprinted by permission of Harcourt Brace Jovanovich, Inc.

Harper & Row, Publishers, Inc.: For "Trucks," "Underground Rumbling," and "Tugs" from *I Go A-Traveling* by James S. Tippett. Copyright, 1929, by Harper & Row, Publishers. Copyright renewed 1957 by James S. Tippett. Reprinted by permission of Harper & Row, Publishers, Inc.

D. C. Heath and Company: For "Trains at Night" by Frances M. Frost from *The Packet*. Reprinted by permission of the Publisher.

Holt, Rinehart and Winston, Inc.: For "Bus Stop" from *Is Somewhere Always Far Away?* by Leland B. Jacobs. Copyright © 1967 by Leland B. Jacobs. Reprinted by permission of Holt, Rinehart and Winston, Inc. For "Steam Shovel" from *Upper Pasture: Poems by Charles Malam*. Copyright 1930, 1958 by Charles Malam. Reprinted by permission of Holt, Rinehart and Winston, Inc.

Houghton Mifflin Company: For "Whenever the stars are out of sight" by Ruth Harnden from *Wonder Why*. Copyright © 1971 by Ruth P. Harnden. Reprinted by permission of Houghton Mifflin Company.

Index of Authors